KT-170-160

Tips for Reading Together

Children learn best when reading is fun.

- Talk about the title and the picture on the front cover.
- Discuss what you think the story might be about.
- Read the story together, inviting your child to read as much of it as they can.
- Give lots of praise as your child reads, and help them when necessary.
- If they get stuck, try reading the first sound of the word, or break the word into chunks, or read the whole sentence again. Focus on the meaning.
- Re-read the story later, encouraging your child to read as much of it as they can.

Children enjoy re-reading stories and this helps to build their confidence.

Have fun!

After you have read the story, find the 7 hidden keys, and the letters and letter shapes that make up the word TRAPPED.

This book includes these useful common words:
very   must   look(ed)   pulled   suddenly

For more hints and tips on helping your child become a successful and enthusiastic reader look at our website www.oxfordowl.co.uk.

Trapped!

Written by Cynthia Rider
based on the original characters
created by Roderick Hunt and Alex Brychta
Illustrated by Alex Brychta

OXFORD
UNIVERSITY PRESS

Please return
the key

Keep dogs
on a lead

Gran took the children and
Floppy to see an old castle.

The children went up the path to
the castle. Suddenly, Chip stopped.

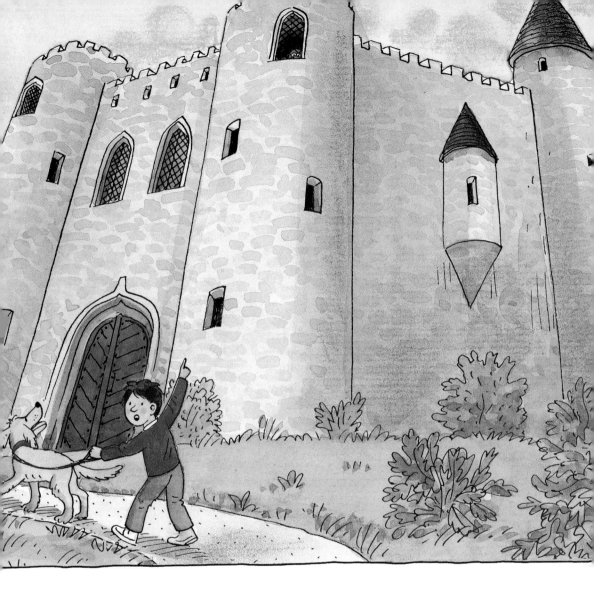

He pointed to a window at the top.
"Look, there's a face," he said.

Everyone looked, but the face
had gone.

"It can't be a face," said Gran.
"The castle is empty."

They went into the castle.

"It looks very old," said Biff.

"And very scary!" said Kipper.

"Let's play hide and seek," said Chip.

The children ran in and out of the rooms.

"I'll play too," said Gran, and
she went into the next room.

Gran looked for a place to hide.
She saw a gate and pulled it open.

CLANG! The gate banged shut.

Gran pushed it, but it was stuck.

"Help! Help!" she shouted.

The children ran to see what had happened.

"I'm trapped," said Gran.

The gate was very stiff.

The children pulled and pulled.

At last, it opened.

"I'll keep the gate open with this old chest," said Gran. "I don't want to be trapped again."

"Come on," said Kipper. "Let's see
where these stairs go."

They all went up the stairs.

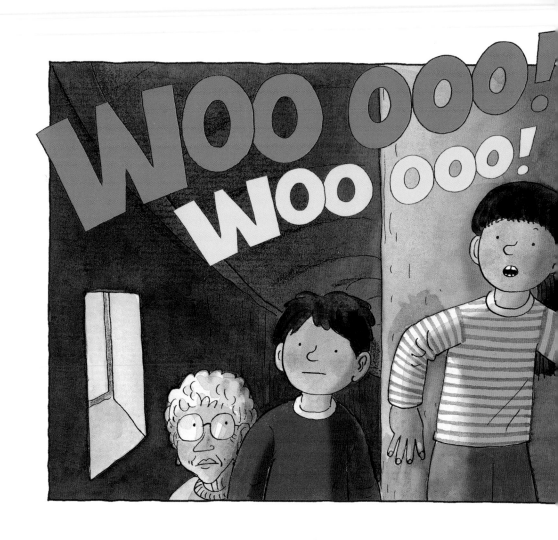

Suddenly, they heard a noise.

Woo...ooo! WOO...OOO!

"What was that?" said Biff.

The noise came again.

Woo...ooo! WOO...OOO!

Floppy pulled at his lead and
raced up the stairs.

"Come on! We must go after Floppy," said Chip. They all ran to the top of the stairs.

Floppy was scratching at a small
door. Gran slowly turned the
handle.

They saw a small dusty room.
"Come on, Floppy," said Biff.
"Let's have a look around."

Something went flapping across
the room.

"What's that?" said Biff.

Chip pointed. "It's an owl," he
whispered. "It must be the face I
saw at the window."

"Poor thing! It must have come down the chimney," said Gran. She picked it up very gently.

Gran took the owl over to the
window and opened it. The owl
blinked its big round eyes.

"Go on, owl," said
Kipper. "Fly away!"
The owl flapped
its wings and flew
up into the sky.

Kipper watched the owl fly away.
"It must be horrible to be trapped,"
he said.

"It is, Kipper," said Gran. "It is!"

Talk about the story

Why did Chip think he had seen a face at the window?

Why did Gran call to the children for help?

Why did Gran keep the gate open with the chest?

What would you do if you found a trapped animal?

Rhyming pairs

Find the four pairs of things that rhyme.
Which is the odd pair out?

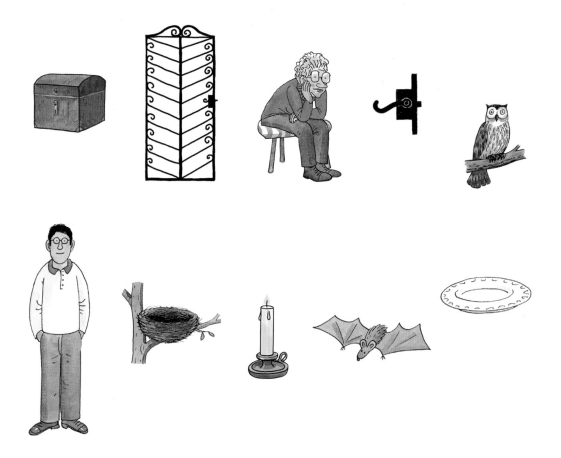

Read with Biff, Chip and Kipper offers two important pathways to learning to read. **First Stories** have been specially written to provide practice in reading everyday language, and the **Phonics** stories help children practise reading by decoding sounds in words, as they learn to do in school.

Books at Level 5: Building confidence in reading

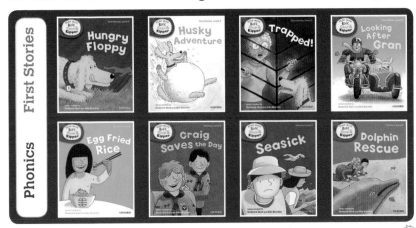

Look out for the next level: Reading with confidence

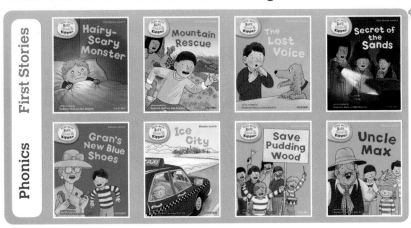

OXFORD
UNIVERSITY PRESS

Great Clarendon Street, Oxford OX2 6DP
Text © Cynthia Rider 2006
Illustrations © Alex Brychta 2006
First published 2006. This edition published 2011
10 9 8 7 6 5

Series Editors: Kate Ruttle, Annemarie Young
Designed by Andy Wilson
British Library Cataloguing in Publication Data available
ISBN: 978-0-19-274571-2
Printed in China by Imago
The characters in this work are the original creation of
Roderick Hunt and Alex Brychta who retain copyright
in the characters.